204
Fergus Falls, MN 56538-0717

HARRIET and the

GARDEN

HARRIET and the GARDEN

· GARDEN ·

Nancy Carlson

Carolrhoda Books, Inc. ◆ Minneapolis

for John and Margie Ligon, because they've
been loyal fans and so much help with my work,
and for Josie, because her creativity is an inspiration!

This book is available in two editions:
Library binding by Carolrhoda Books, Inc.
Soft cover by First Avenue Editions, 1997
c/o The Lerner Publishing Group
241 First Avenue North
Minneapolis, Minnesota 55401

Copyright © 1982 by CAROLRHODA BOOKS, INC.

All rights reserved. International copyright secured.
No part of this book may be reproduced in any form whatsoever
without permission in writing from the publisher except for
the inclusion of brief quotations in an acknowledged review.

LIBRARY OF CONGRESS CATALOGING IN PUBLICATION DATA

Carlson, Nancy L.
    Harriet and the garden.

    Summary: Harriet feels terrible until she
confesses to trampling on a neighbor's garden
and ruining a prize dahlia.
    [1. Garden — Fiction. 2. Honesty — Fiction.
3. Dogs — Fiction] I. Title.
PZ7.C21665Han   [E]   81-18136
ISBN 0-87614-184-X (lib. bdg.)
ISBN 1-57505-065-X (pbk.)

Manufactured in the United States of America
5 6 7 8 9 10 – P/JP – 02 01 00 99 98 97

It was a beautiful summer day. Harriet was
playing ball with some pals.

Across the park, Mrs. Hoozit was working in her garden.

Mrs. Hoozit had been waiting for this day for a long time. Her prize dahlia was in full bloom. "I must call the garden club and have them come over today and have a look," she said.

Meanwhile, Harriet was playing outfield.

Suddenly George hit a fly ball. Harriet just had to catch it. If she didn't, it would be a home run for sure.

Harriet ran back and back. She kept her eyes
on the ball. She was concentrating so hard
that she never even noticed when she came to
Mrs. Hoozit's garden.

She ran backward right through the perfect
mums. Then she trampled through the lilies.

In the middle of the rose bushes she caught
the ball.

And then she fell down right on top of the
prize dahlia in full bloom.
"Oops," said Harriet.
"Let's get out of here," said her pals.

Everyone ran except for Harriet. She looked around her at the garden. Everything was ruined.

Suddenly Harriet heard Mrs. Hoozit's voice.
"What's happened to my beautiful garden?"

Harriet was so scared that she just took off.
She ran and she ran and she never turned
back.

Harriet ran all the way home, up the stairs, and into her bedroom. She slammed the door.

Maybe she didn't recognize me, thought
Harriet.

But she decided she'd better spend the rest of
the day inside.

"Are you all right, Harriet?" Mother asked.

"Just fine," said Harriet.

That night Harriet couldn't eat her supper.

Her favorite television program wasn't very interesting.

She didn't even care when Mother made
popcorn balls.

When Harriet went to bed, she couldn't sleep.

And when she finally fell asleep, she had bad dreams.

The next morning Harriet made a decision.

She went straight to Mrs. Hoozit's house and confessed.

Then she spent the rest of the day helping
Mrs. Hoozit plant new flowers and tie up the
broken rose bushes. They had a good time.

When Harriet got home, she was a mess.

"Harriet, are you all right?" Mother asked.

"Just fine!" said Harriet.